MARVEL

GUARDIANS OF THE GALAXY VOL. 2

marvelkids.com

© 2017 MARVEL.

Illustrations by Ron Lim, Andy Smith, Andy Troy, and Chris Sotomayor

Cover design by Elaine Lopez-Levine. Cover illustration by Ron Lim, Andy Smith, Andy Troy, and Chris Sotomayor

Little, Brown and Company
Hachette Book Group
1290 Avenue of the Americas, New York, NY 10104
Visit us at lb-kids.com
marvelkids.com

First Edition: April 2017

Little, Brown and Company is a division of Hachette Book Group, Inc.
The Little, Brown name and logo are trademarks of Hachette Book Group, Inc.

The publisher is not responsible for websites (or their content) that are not owned by the publisher.

ISBNs: 978-0-316-27161-5 (pbk.), 978-0-316-55394-0 (ebook), 978-0-316-55393-3 (ebook), 978-0-316-31417-6 (ebook)

Printed in the United States of America

CW

10 9 8 7 6 5 4 3 2

MARVEL

GUARDIANS OF THE GALAXY VOL. 2

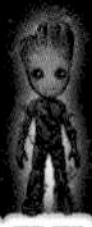

REVENGE OF THE RAVAGERS

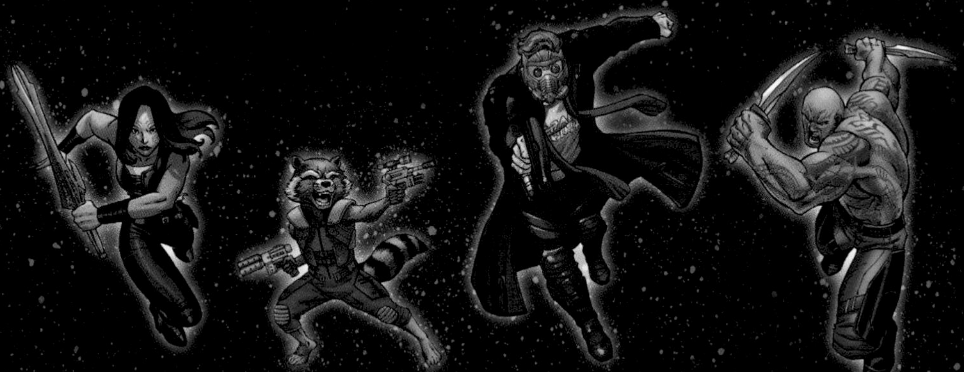

Adapted by R. R. Busse

Illustrations by Ron Lim, Andy Smith, Andy Troy, and Chris Sotomayor

Based on the Major Motion Picture

Produced by Kevin Feige, p.g.a.

Written and Directed by James Gunn

LB

LITTLE, BROWN AND COMPANY

New York Boston

It looks like the Guardians of the Galaxy are in trouble. Peter Quill, Rocket, Groot, Gamora, and Drax desperately try to escape the Sovereign fleet, only moments after completing a successful job for Ayesha, their high priestess and leader.

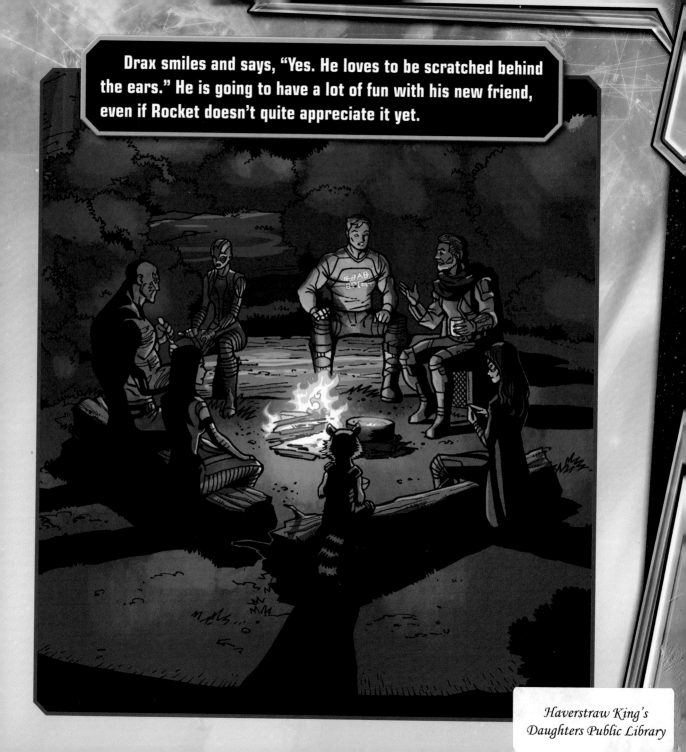

Drax smiles and says, "Yes. He loves to be scratched behind the ears." He is going to have a lot of fun with his new friend, even if Rocket doesn't quite appreciate it yet.

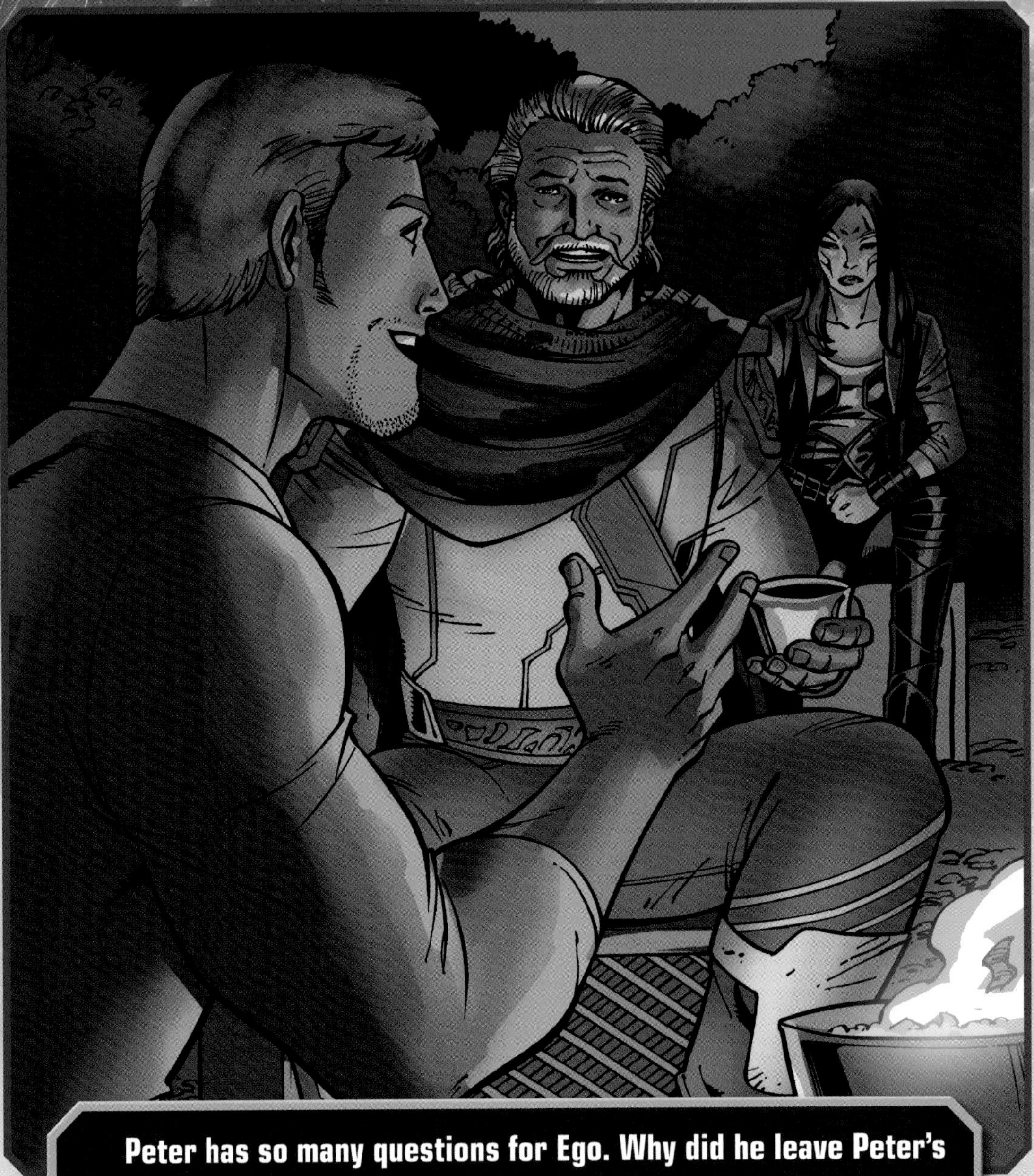

Peter has so many questions for Ego. Why did he leave Peter's mother? Why didn't he claim Peter from the Ravagers? How did Ego find him now? What kind of alien is he, anyway?

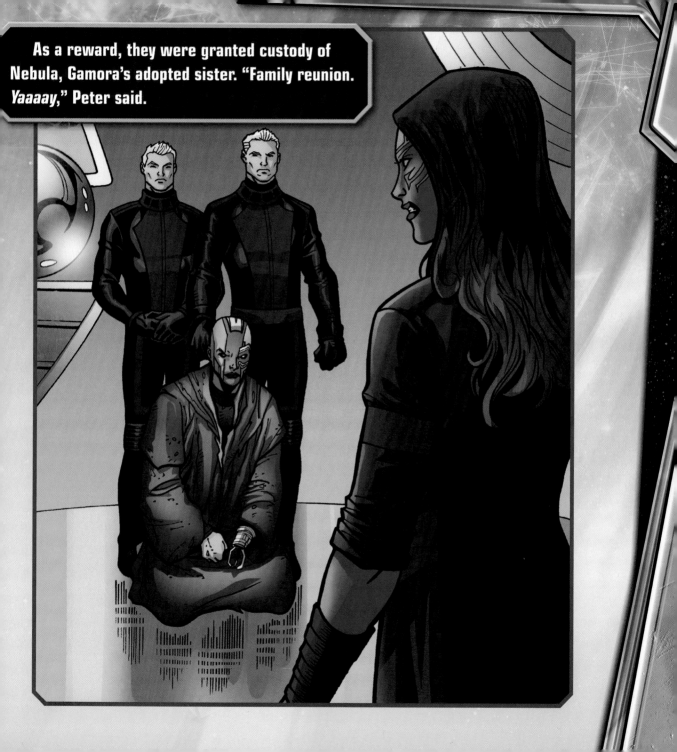

As a reward, they were granted custody of Nebula, Gamora's adopted sister. "Family reunion. *Yaaaay*," Peter said.

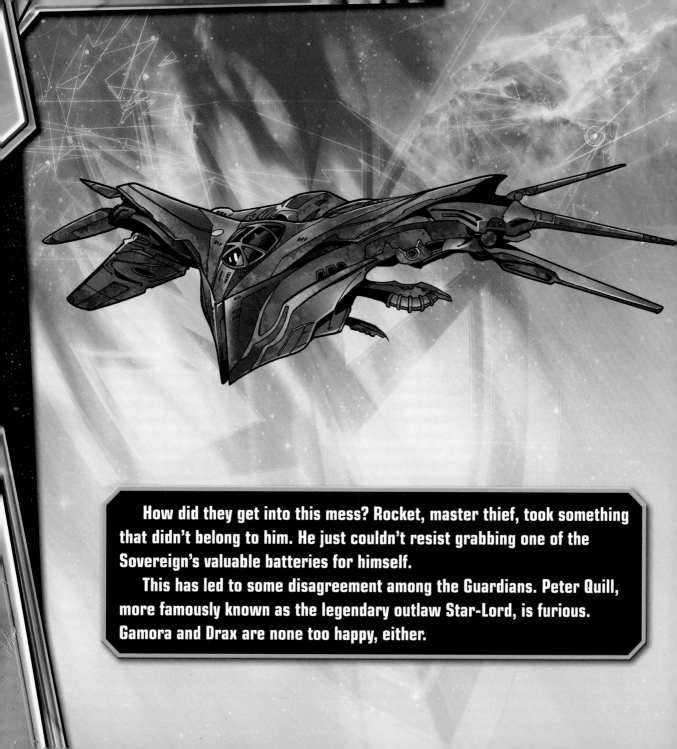

How did they get into this mess? Rocket, master thief, took something that didn't belong to him. He just couldn't resist grabbing one of the Sovereign's valuable batteries for himself.

This has led to some disagreement among the Guardians. Peter Quill, more famously known as the legendary outlaw Star-Lord, is furious. Gamora and Drax are none too happy, either.

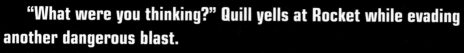

"What were you thinking?" Quill yells at Rocket while evading another dangerous blast.

Rocket shrugs. "Dude, they were really easy to steal," he explains.

"Can everyone just put the bickering on hold until after we survive the massive space battle?" Gamora scolds.

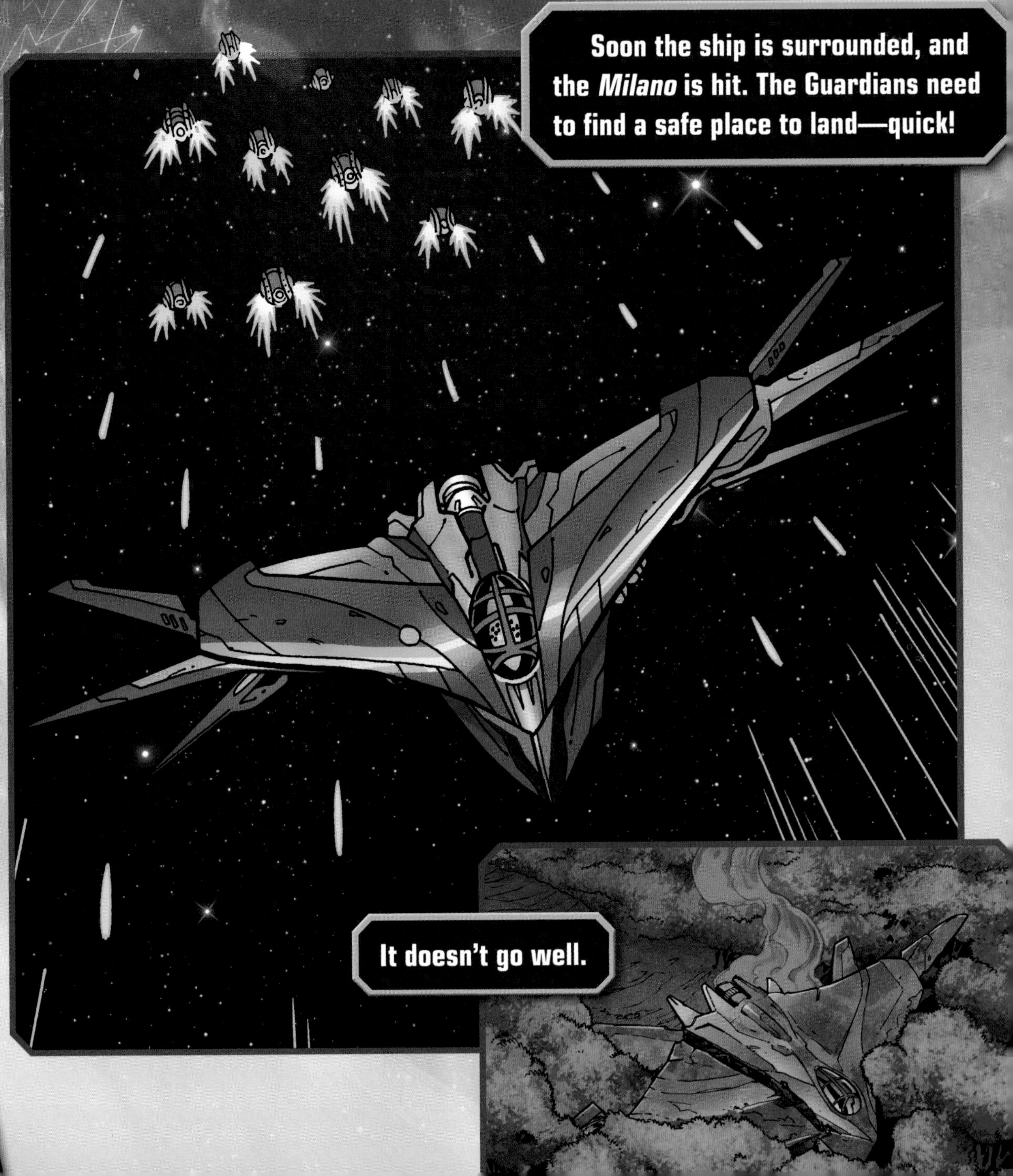
Soon the ship is surrounded, and the *Milano* is hit. The Guardians need to find a safe place to land—quick!
It doesn't go well.

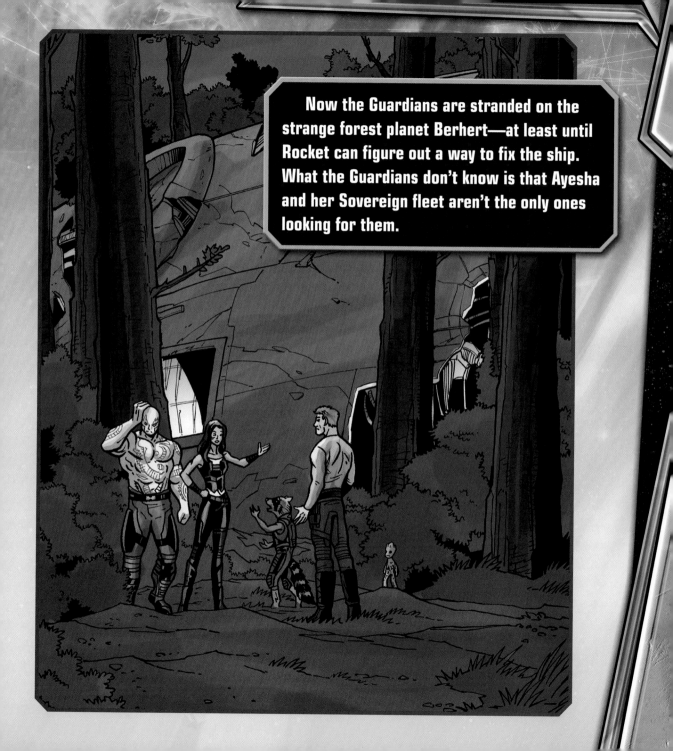

Now the Guardians are stranded on the strange forest planet Berhert—at least until Rocket can figure out a way to fix the ship. What the Guardians don't know is that Ayesha and her Sovereign fleet aren't the only ones looking for them.

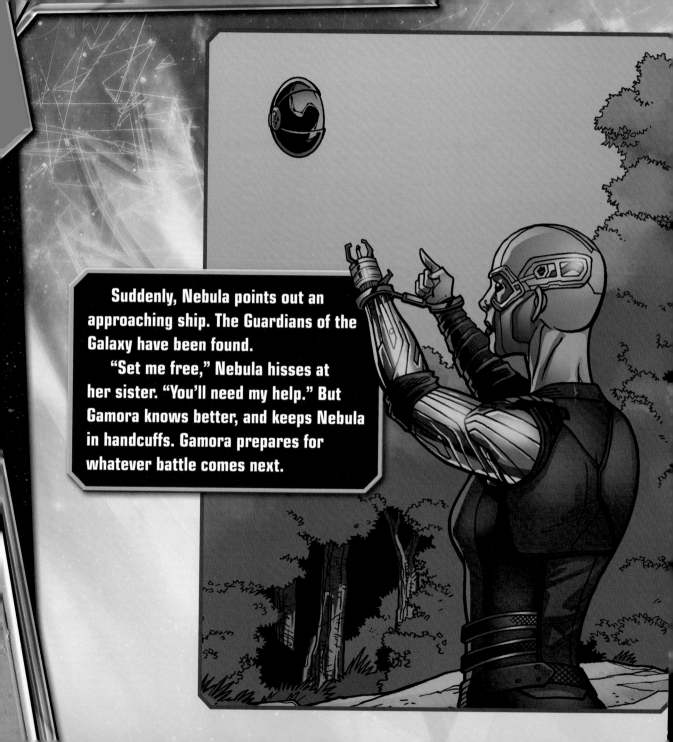

Suddenly, Nebula points out an approaching ship. The Guardians of the Galaxy have been found.

"Set me free," Nebula hisses at her sister. "You'll need my help." But Gamora knows better, and keeps Nebula in handcuffs. Gamora prepares for whatever battle comes next.

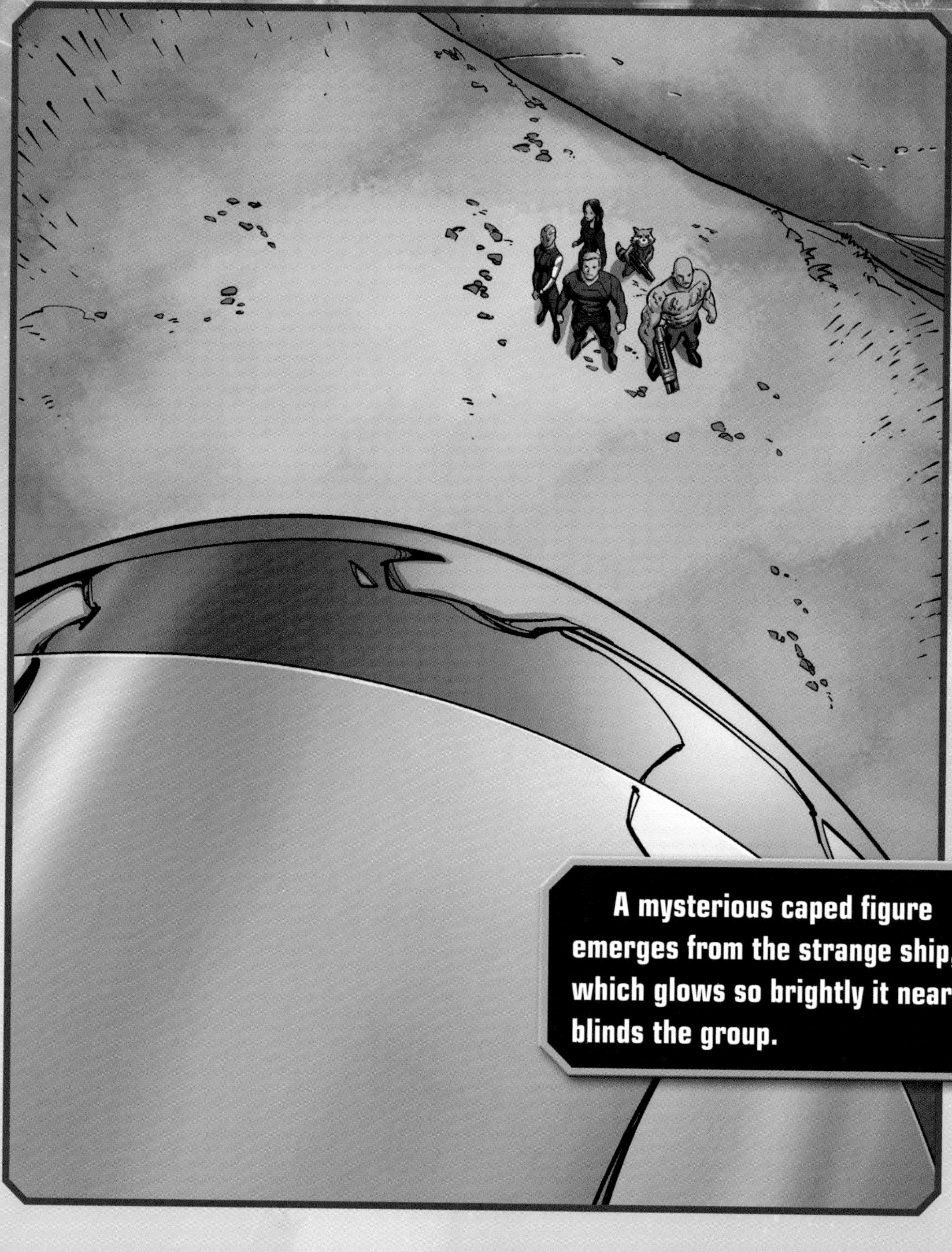
A mysterious caped figure emerges from the strange ship, which glows so brightly it nearly blinds the group.

As the man approaches, the Guardians raise their weapons and demand to know who he is. "I figured my rugged good looks would make it obvious to you, even after thirty years. My name's Ego," he says, "and I'm your dad, Peter."

The Guardians are shocked.

The woman with him is named Mantis. She doesn't say much, but seems to form a bond with the Guardians—mostly Drax. "Can I pet your puppy?" she asks Drax, pointing at Rocket. "It is adorable!"

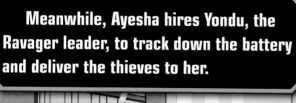

Meanwhile, Ayesha hires Yondu, the Ravager leader, to track down the battery and deliver the thieves to her.

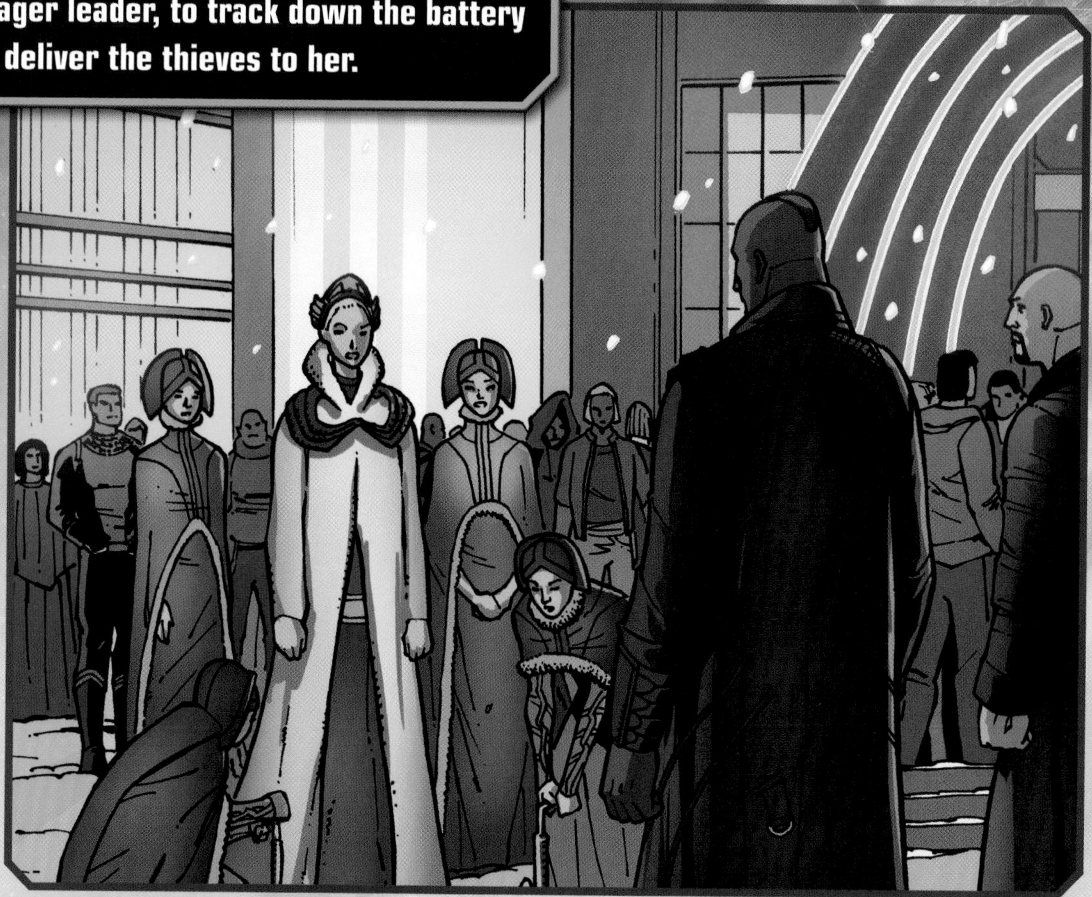

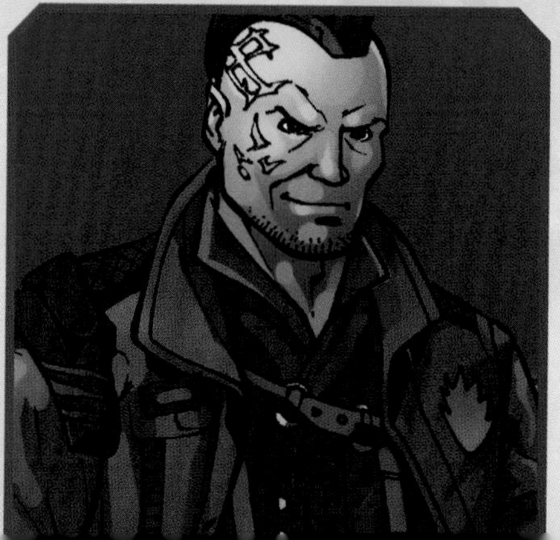

Yondu originally abducted Peter from Earth, but then raised him as a surrogate son. Yondu's frequent too-tough love wore thin on Peter, and they went their separate ways.

Gamora is not too trusting of this new man claiming to be Peter's father. "We have no reason to believe he's actually your father," Gamora says as patiently as possible. But Peter seems so driven that she eventually agrees to leave with Ego, Mantis, and Drax to get proof of their relationship.

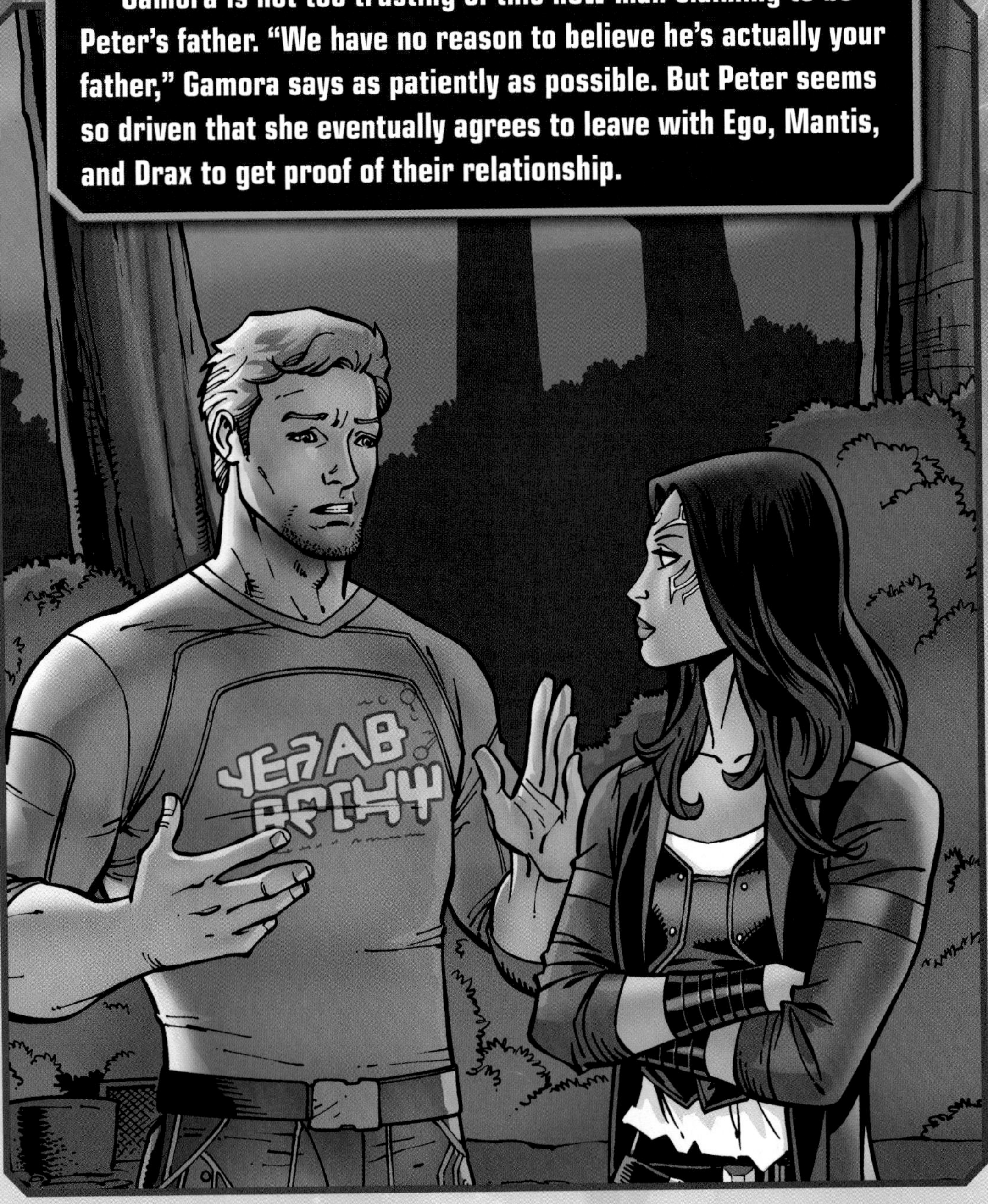

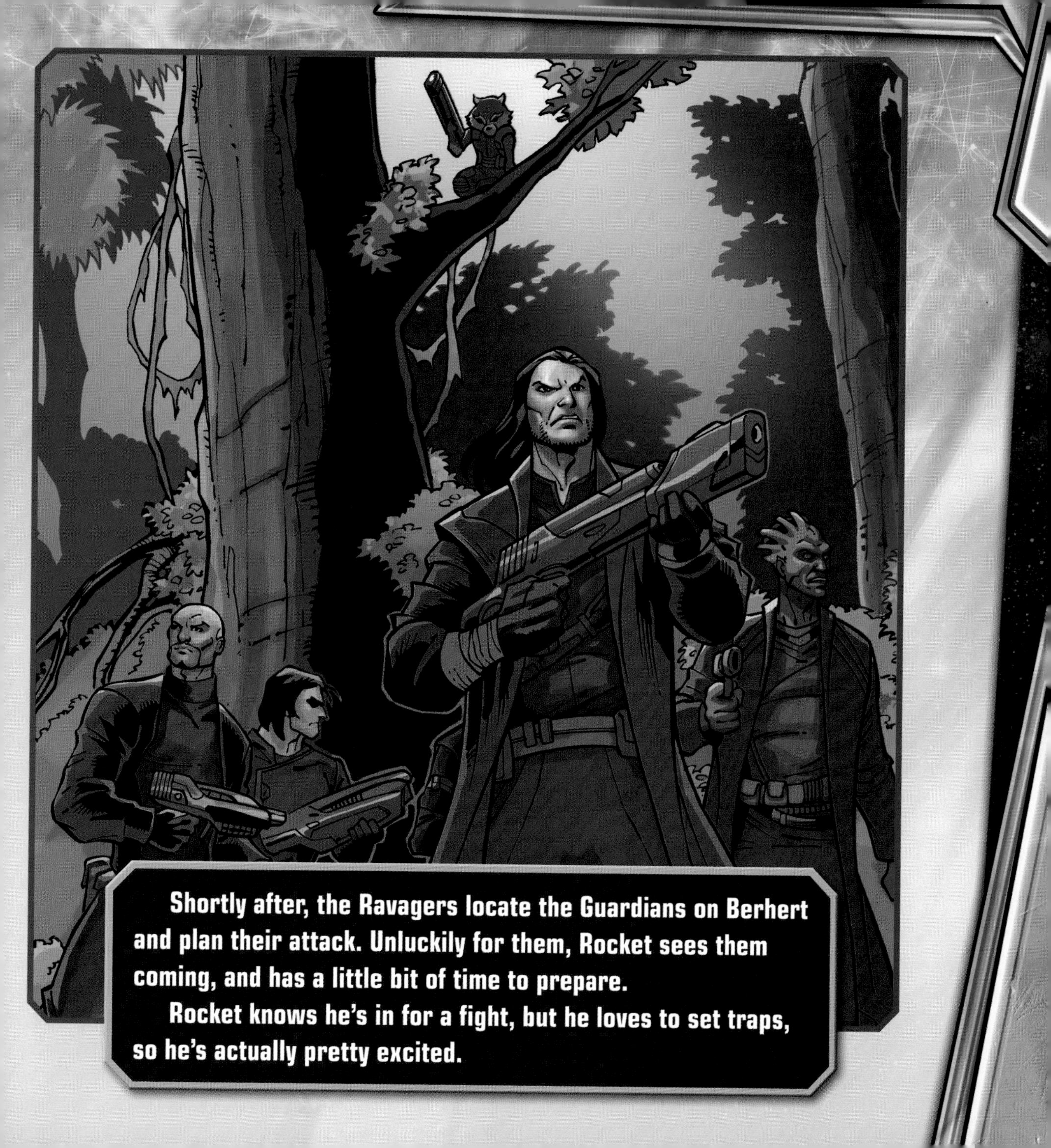

Shortly after, the Ravagers locate the Guardians on Berhert and plan their attack. Unluckily for them, Rocket sees them coming, and has a little bit of time to prepare.

Rocket knows he's in for a fight, but he loves to set traps, so he's actually pretty excited.

Rocket jumps from his hiding place and attacks. "Here ya go, fellas. Lemme get those for ya," he says as he disarms a group of Ravagers.

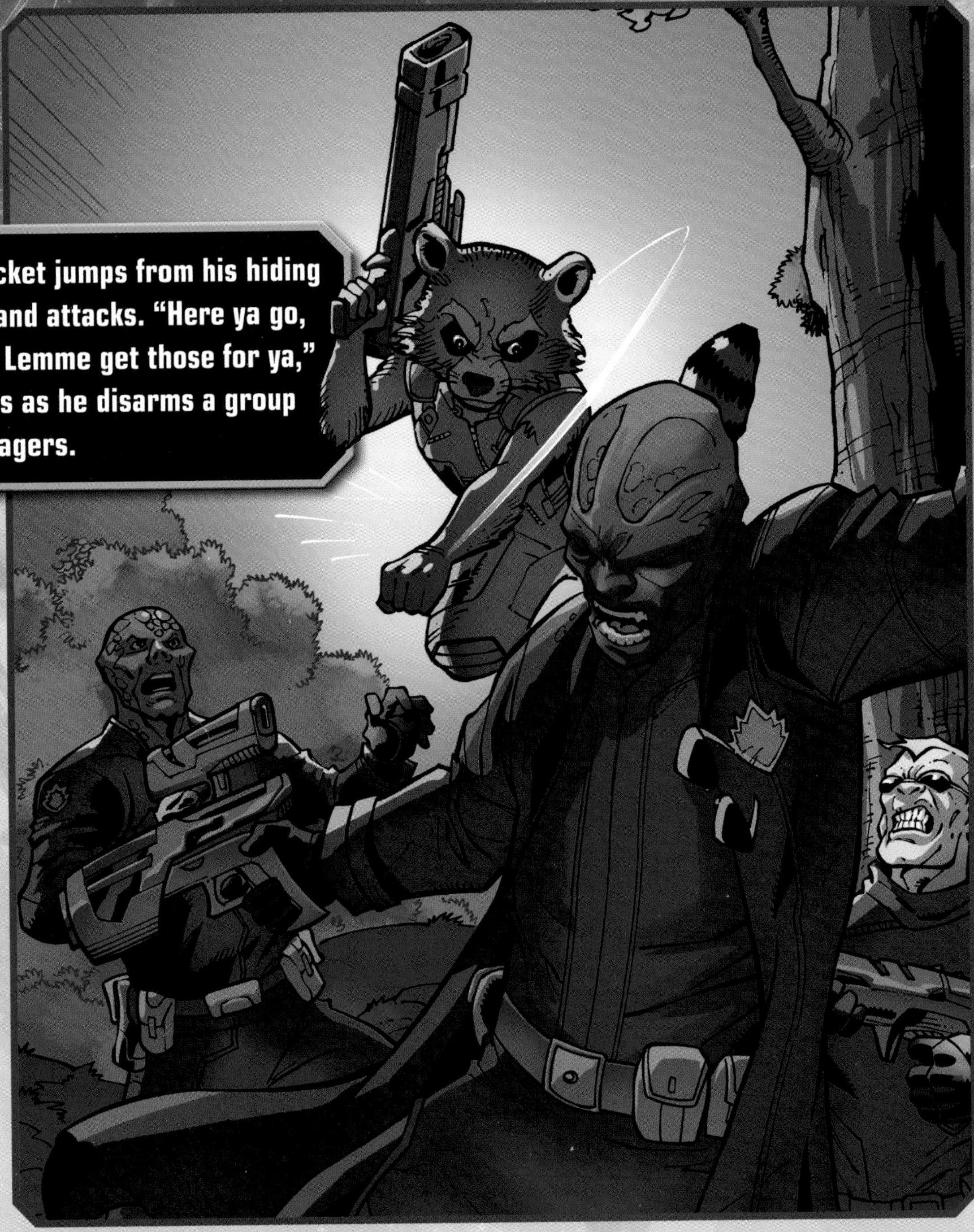

Rocket is so busy having fun, he doesn't notice two big Ravagers sneaking up on him. At the last second, he leaps into the air and flips behind one! Rocket seems like he's having fun again...

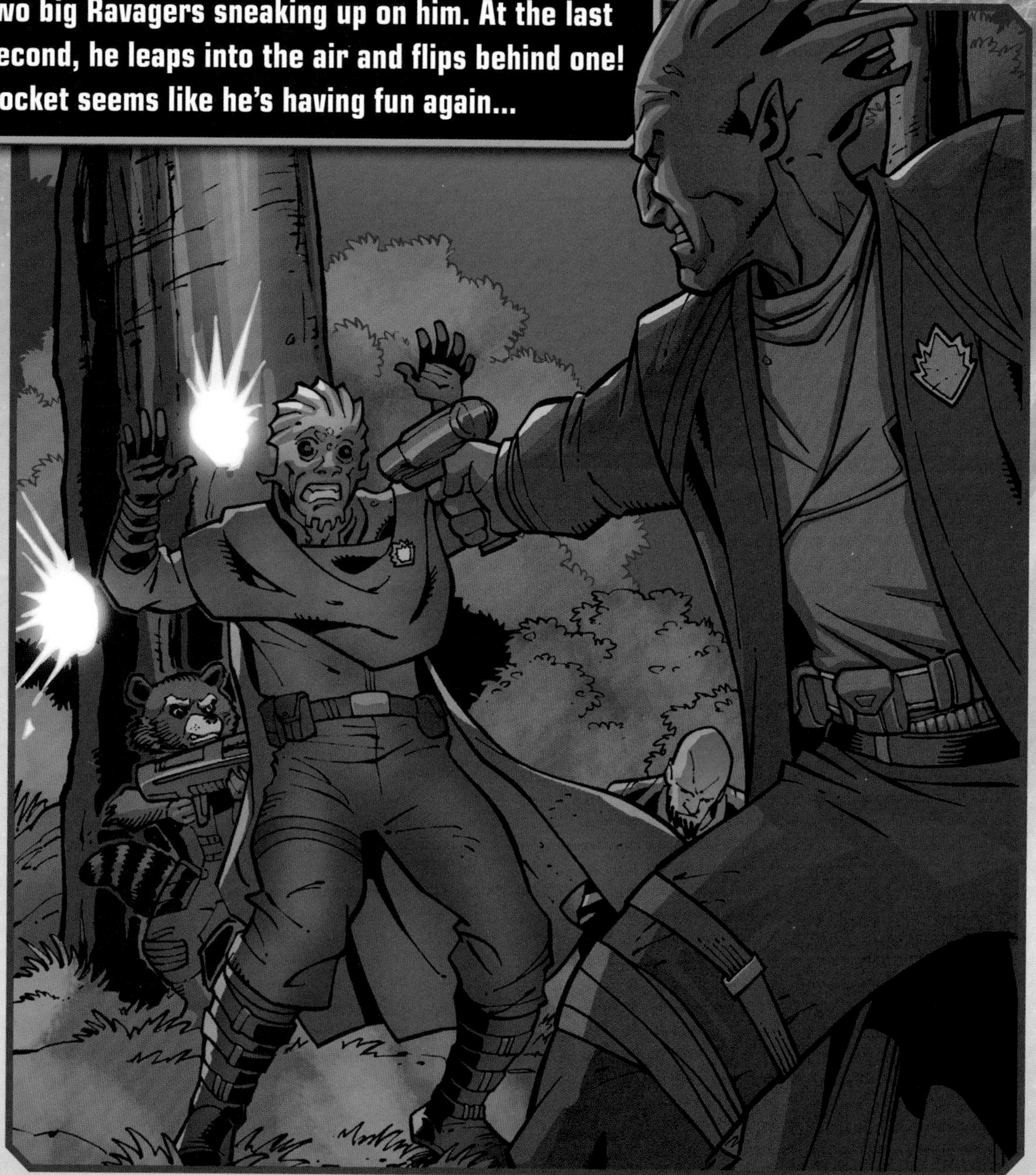

...until Yondu shows up, that is, with reinforcements. Now all Rocket can hope to do is cause enough of a distraction that the other Guardians come back for him—or Groot comes to the rescue.

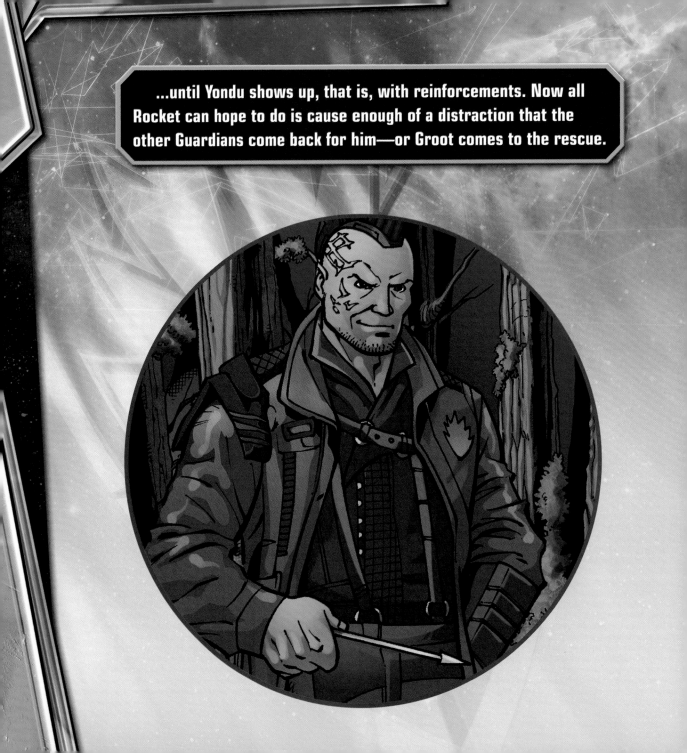

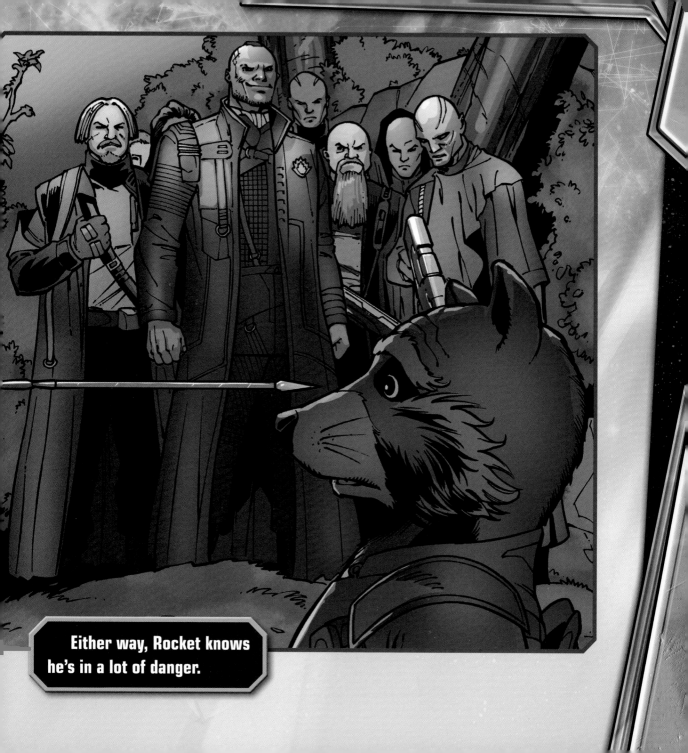

Either way, Rocket knows he's in a lot of danger.

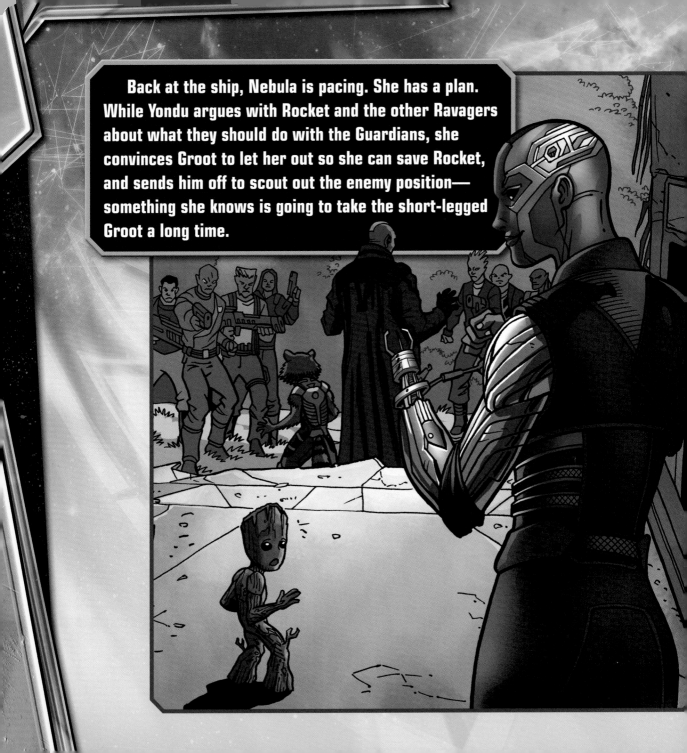

Back at the ship, Nebula is pacing. She has a plan. While Yondu argues with Rocket and the other Ravagers about what they should do with the Guardians, she convinces Groot to let her out so she can save Rocket, and sends him off to scout out the enemy position—something she knows is going to take the short-legged Groot a long time.

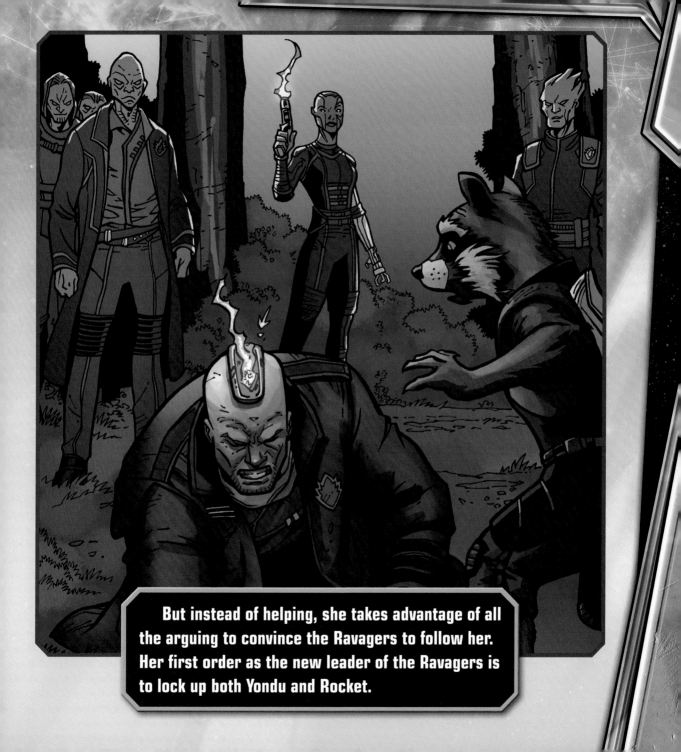

But instead of helping, she takes advantage of all the arguing to convince the Ravagers to follow her. Her first order as the new leader of the Ravagers is to lock up both Yondu and Rocket.

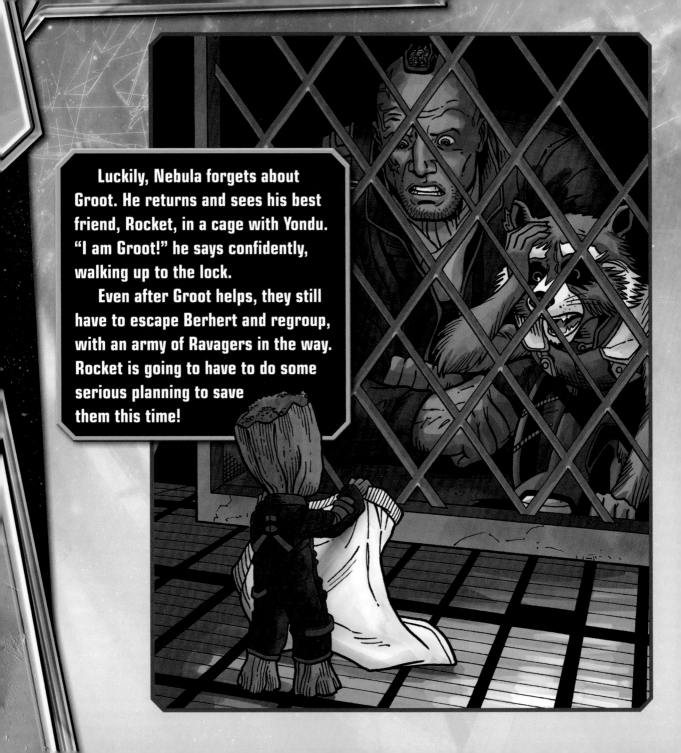

Luckily, Nebula forgets about Groot. He returns and sees his best friend, Rocket, in a cage with Yondu. "I am Groot!" he says confidently, walking up to the lock.

Even after Groot helps, they still have to escape Berhert and regroup, with an army of Ravagers in the way. Rocket is going to have to do some serious planning to save them this time!